Elephant on the Loose

by Kim Watson

illustrated by Sheree Boyd

Simon Spotlight/Nick Jr.

New York   London   Toronto   Sydney   Singapore

Based on the TV series *Little Bill*® created by Bill Cosby as seen on Nick Jr.®

SIMON SPOTLIGHT
An imprint of Simon & Schuster Children's Publishing Division
1230 Avenue of the Americas, New York, New York 10020
Copyright © 2001 Viacom International Inc. All rights reserved.
NICKELODEON, NICK JR., and all related titles, logos, and characters are trademarks of
Viacom International Inc. *Little Bill* is a trademark of Smiley, Inc.
All rights reserved including the right of reproduction in whole or in part in any form.
SIMON SPOTLIGHT and colophon are registered trademarks of Simon & Schuster.
Manufactured in the United States of America
First Edition
10 9 8 7 6 5 4 3 2 1
ISBN 0-689-84083-7

It was a beautiful morning. Little Bill stretched and yawned, and then he waved at his pet hamster, Elephant, in his cage.

"Good morning!" Little Bill exclaimed.

He could hardly wait to play with Elephant.

Little Bill put Elephant inside his exercise ball and began to sing, "Elephant's a hamster, he's my pet. He's my pet and the greatest hamster yet."

As he sang, Elephant rolled around Little Bill's feet.

"That's a nice song, Little Bill," Brenda said, poking her head into the room. "But you'd better get dressed now if you want to go get some new sneakers."

"Yippee!" Little Bill shouted. "Mama, can Elephant come?"

"Not unless he needs sneakers too," Brenda answered, smiling. Then she walked away singing,

"Elephant's my hamster . . ."

"Come here, Elephant," Little Bill called. "I have to put you back in your cage before I go."

But before Little Bill could scoop him up, Elephant zigzagged across the room and got away.

"Elephant, come here," Little Bill pleaded.

But Elephant didn't come.

Little Bill grabbed a box of hamster treats and gave it a shake. They were Elephant's favorite snack.

"Okay, Elephant. Come and get it," Little Bill called out.

Elephant rolled his ball into Little Bill's hand and Little Bill gave Elephant his snack.

Little Bill got dressed in a hurry.

"Elephant's my hamster. I think he's the best. He's even better than the rest," Little Bill sang as he put on his pants. He sang as he tied his shoes. And he was *still* singing as he put on his shirt.

While Little Bill sang, Elephant gobbled up his treats.

Finally, Little Bill looked in the mirror.

"There!" he said with a satisfied grin. "I'm ready to go."

Suddenly he stopped.

"Oops!" he exclaimed. "I forgot to put Elephant back in his cage."

But when Little Bill turned around, Elephant was gone.

Little Bill searched high and low. "Come out, come out, wherever you are!" he yelled.

"Elephant!" he called. "I don't have time to play hide-and-seek."

But he couldn't find Elephant anywhere!

"Come on, Little Bill! It's time to go!" April called.

"I can't find Elephant!" Little Bill confided.

"You mean he ran away?" Bobby asked.

"Ran away? Where would he go?" Little Bill asked.

Bobby answered, "If the front door is open, he could be halfway around the world by now."

"Around the world?" Little Bill said, full of worry.

"Yep. He could be anywhere," said Bobby.

Suddenly Little Bill imagined
he was searching the plains of a
distant land.

"There must be a ka-billion
animals here," he said to himself.
"How am I going to find
Elephant?"

Little Bill looked at Elephant's empty cage and ran from the room as fast as he could.

"Mama! Dad! Alice the Great!" he cried. "Close all the doors! Close all the doors!" he shouted with arms flailing and legs churning.

Little Bill ran so fast that he could barely catch his breath. "Elephant ran away!" he told his family. "He's gone."

"But, Little Bill, he was just in your room," Brenda said.

"He must be somewhere in this house," Big Bill reassured him. "All the doors are closed."

Just then April and Bobby came running down the stairs.

"He's not in your room, Little Bill!" April exclaimed.

"Let's split up and search the whole house," said Big Bill.

"I'll get my detective gear and look for clues," Bobby declared.

"We'll find that little rascal!" Alice the Great announced.

Little Bill felt a little better.

Everyone ran in different directions.

"Elephant! Oh, Elephant!" they called. "Elephant, where are you?"

They searched every room and closet. They looked under every chair and table. But still, there was no Elephant!

"Elephant, this isn't very funny. Come on out!" Little Bill yelled.

Elephant had never run away before. "My best friend is gone," Little Bill whispered.

When they finished searching,
everyone went to Little Bill's room.
No one knew what to say.

Little Bill looked around sadly. "I'll never find him." He sighed.

"Try not to worry, baby," Brenda said. "Let's wait here awhile and see if Elephant comes back."

"But I just wish I knew where he went!" Little Bill said tearfully.

Brenda put her arm around Little Bill.

"Don't worry, Little Bill! I've got an idea," Bobby said.

"You do?" Little Bill asked.

"Yep. What does Elephant like?" Bobby asked.

"He likes carrots . . . and lettuce . . . ," Little Bill replied, "and hamster treats! He loves it when I shake the box! And when I sing to him."

Little Bill began to sing, "Elephant's a hamster, he's my pet, he's my pet!"

Soon everybody was dancing and singing loudly.

Suddenly Little Bill saw Elephant by the doorway of his room.

"Elephant!" shouted Little Bill as he ran to his hamster. "You came back!"

Big Bill smiled. "He sure likes those treats," he said.

"He sure likes that song," Brenda said with a laugh.

"And he sure likes *me!*" said Little Bill, gently hugging his favorite friend.